T0363274

For Mummy, who just reconciled with peas.

For Daddy and his garden near the big woods. SC

For my parents, who enjoy peas. AL

This edition published in 2009 by Berbay Publishing

www.berbaybooks.com

First published in 2007 by © L'Atelier du Poisson Soluble
Le Prince au Petit Pois, written by Sylvie Chausse and illustrated by Anne Letuffe

English adaptation by Michael Sedunary
Designed by Relish Graphic Design
Edited by Bryony Oliver-Skuse
Printed and bound in China by Everbest Printing

National Library of Australia
Cataloguing-in publication data:
Chausse, Sylvie.
The prince of peas / Sylvie Chausse.
1st ed.
9780980671100 (hbk.)
Princesses--Juvenile fiction.
Princes--Juvenile fiction.
843.914

For primary school children
ISBN 978-0-9806711-0-0

The Prince of Peas

Text

Sylvie Chausse

Illustration

Anne Letuffe

BERBAY
PUBLISHING

Princess Antoinette
has decided to wed.

The idea has been growing
like a **pea** in her head.

"Very well," says her mother,
the good Queen Louise.
"We'll search till we find you
the true Prince
of Peas."

The Princess is confused

by these words of the Queen.

"How shall we find
him?

What does she
mean?"

PARIS
Choisy-le-Roi
Sens
Choisy-le-roi

Antoinette sets off on
her quest for **romance,**
and comes to a town
in the centre
of France

It's the home of Prince Tristan,
a musician of note,

who can dance as he plays
in his dazzling blue coat.

The Princess writes home to her
mother, the Queen:

"He's the **handsomest**
prince that I've ever seen."

Versailles
Choisy-le-Roi

The Queen sees her daughter is thinking of marriage, so she calls to her footman to bring round the carriage.

They drive to the market where, by royal decree, the footman must purchase a single green pea.

Back home at the palace the Queen hides that pea under seven thick mattresses where no one can see.

For this is the Queen's special **pea test:**
"Let the sleeping prince squash it
to prove he's **the best"**.

That night there's **a party,** with a fabulous band,
Tristan plays - but forgets to hold Antoinette's hand.

At midnight
the Prince goes up to his room ...

... but when he sees all those mattresses, his heart fills with gloom.

He **teeters** on top in his crown and his tights,

crying "Surely they know that my dog can't stand **heights!**"

When he's **gone** the next morning the Princess must agree,

the wedding to Tristan is not meant to be.

Handsome Prince Tristan has failed the **pea test,**

so Princess Antoinette must continue her quest.

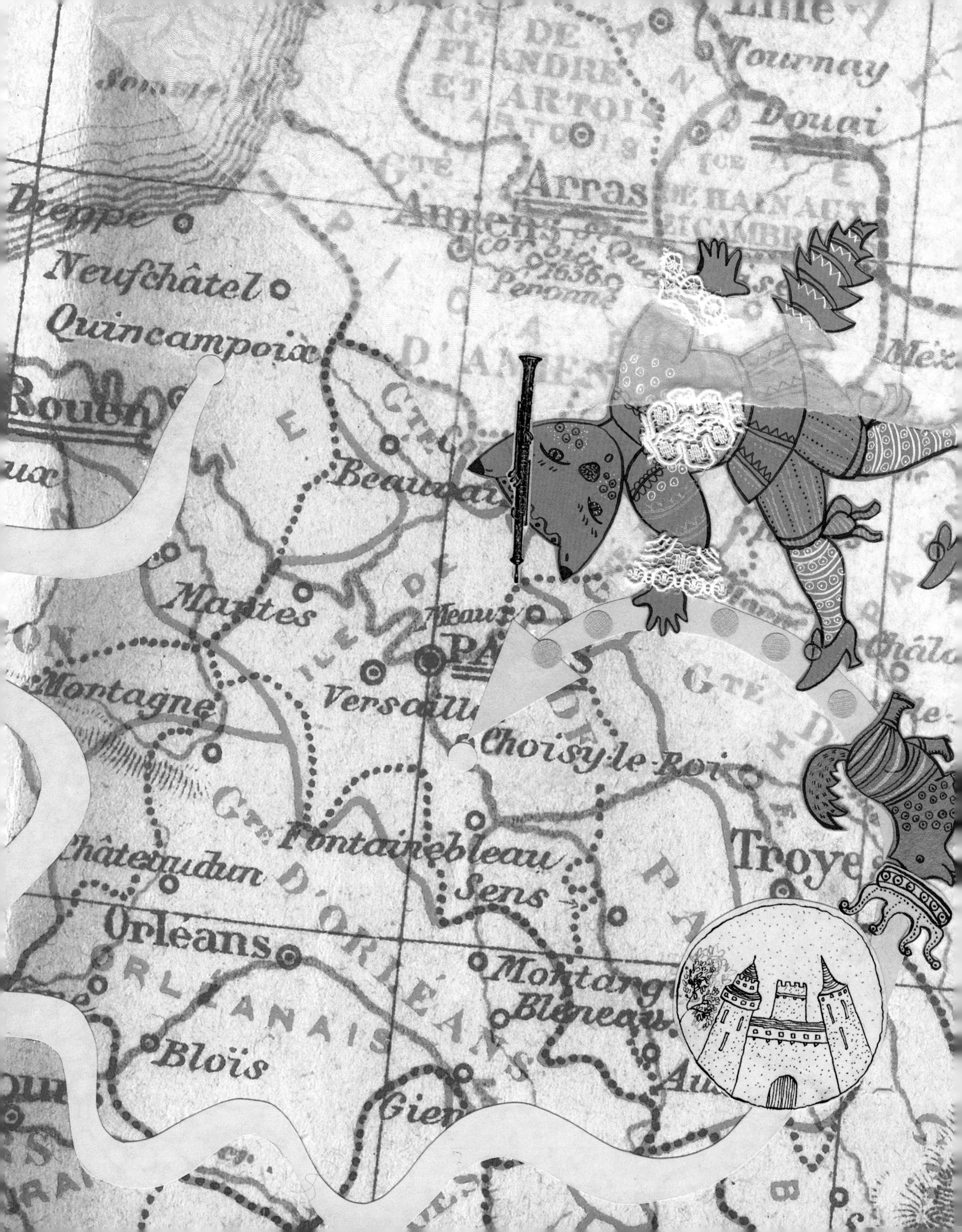
Tournay
Douai
DE
FLANDRE
ET ARTOIS
Arras
Amiens
Dieppe
Neufchâtel
Quincampoix
Rouen
Beauvais
Mantes
Meaux
Versailles
Choisy-le-Roi
Montagne
Fontainebleau
Sens
Châteaudun
Troye
Orléans
Bleneau
Blois
Gien

She meets dashing
Prince Victor whose
skill with the lance

has helped him
win tournaments all
over France.

Antoinette sends a note
with news of her beau,

the Queen decides quickly:

"To market we go!"

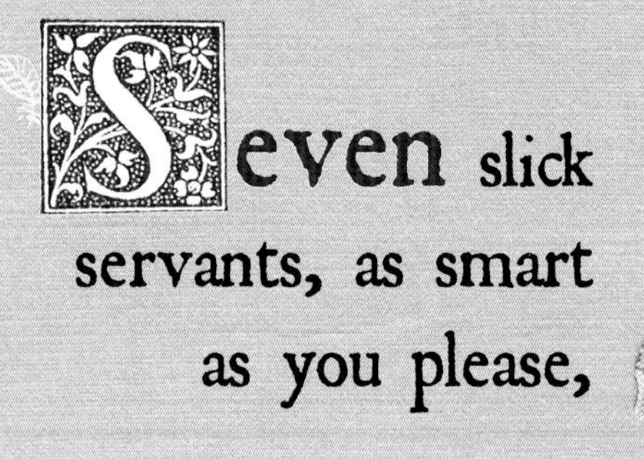

Seven slick
servants, as smart
as you please,

take **seven silk cushions** and buy
seven green peas.

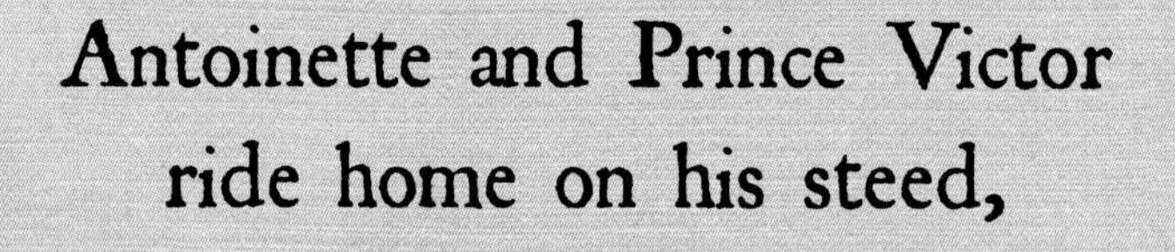

Antoinette and Prince Victor
ride home on his steed,

a right royal couple,
a **fine pair** indeed!

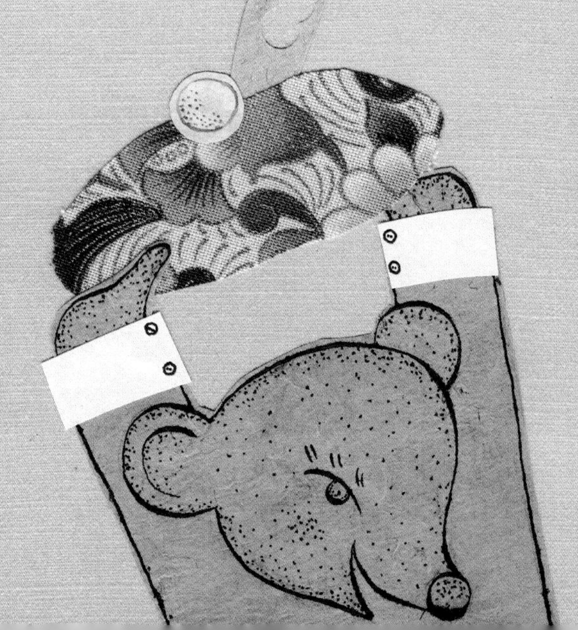

Now there's only one mattress
and seven green peas,
Victor should pass the Queen's
pea test **with ease.**

That night,
what rejoicing,
a feast fit for a king,

but rude, crude
Prince Victor
eats **hardly** a thing.

He goes to his **room**,
sees the thin feather bed,

and decides that he'll sleep
with his **war-horse** instead!

When next morning
they leave,
without thanks or **good-bye,**
Princess Antoinette
just cannot deny ...

her quest for a Prince
has all been in vain.

Does she still have
the **heart**
to go **searching**
again?

The Princess decides to give love one more chance,

And sets off for a town in the deep

south of France ...

where in dangerous waters on the outskirts of town,

an unfortunate cat, seems destined to drown ...

... till brave Prince Philippe
with courage supreme,

rescues the cat from the
treacherous stream.

Princess gazes at Prince,
Prince beams at Princess.

What happens **next?**
Do you **think** you can guess?

A **card** is sent home, on the wings of a dove,

to tell Antoinette's mother she's madly in **love**.

"To market, to Market!" cries good Queen Louise,

and a convoy of servants is sent to buy peas.

They buy peas by the cartload, then their job is to spread, hundreds of peas in Prince Philippe's bed.

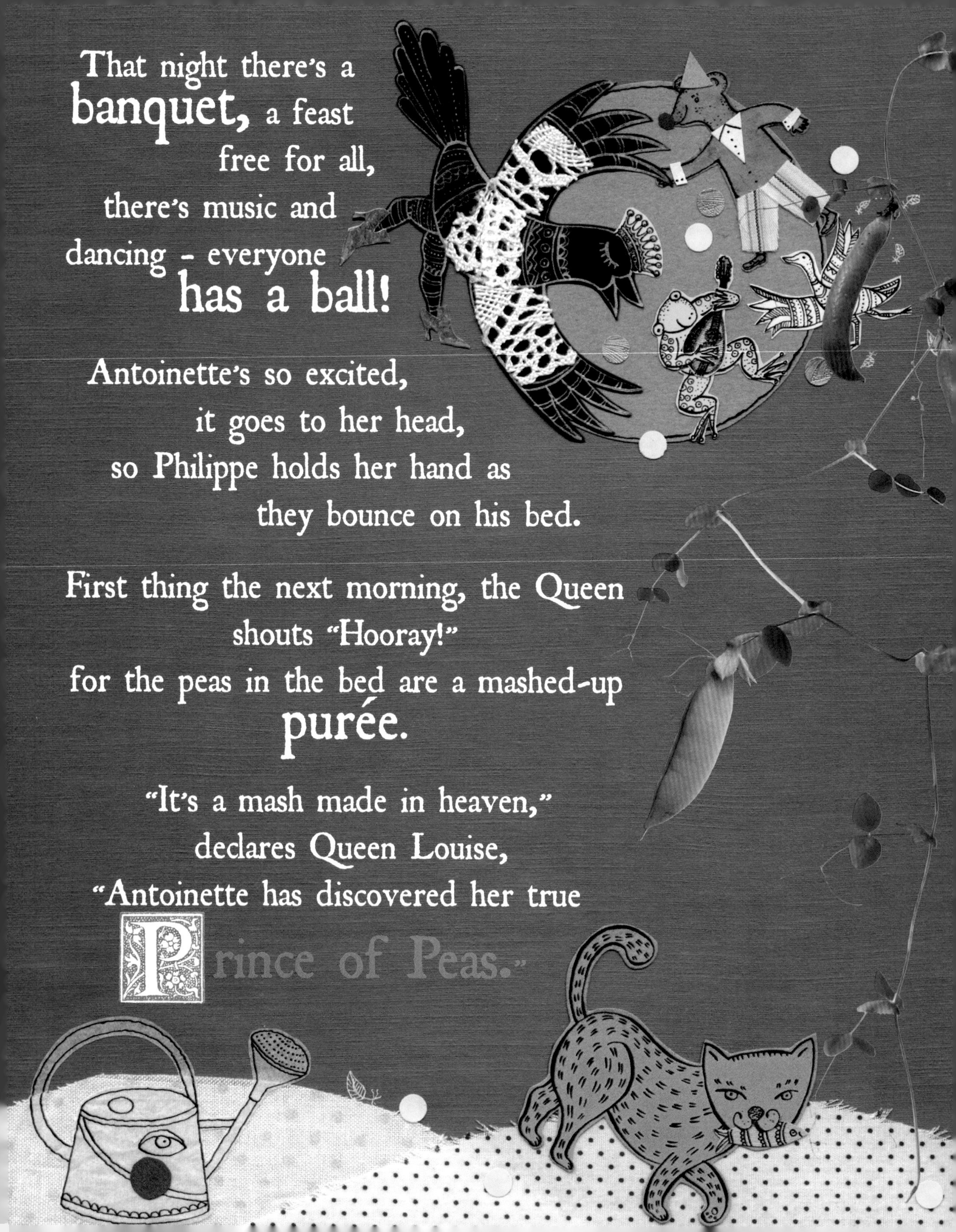

That night there's a **banquet**, a feast free for all,
there's music and dancing - everyone **has a ball!**

Antoinette's so excited, it goes to her head,
so Philippe holds her hand as they bounce on his bed.

First thing the next morning, the Queen shouts "Hooray!"
for the peas in the bed are a mashed-up **purée**.

"It's a mash made in heaven," declares Queen Louise,
"Antoinette has discovered her true Prince of Peas."

It's the
day of the wedding
for Prince and Princess,
and the bride has selected
a **pea-patterned** dress.
Her crown is of sweet peas,
and – here's a
strange thing! –
a special green pea is
the **jewel** in her ring.

Toi et Moi

Antoinette
is so **happy**,
so pleased to be wed,
that another **idea**
takes shape in her head.

The **months**, they pass by,
the idea grows and grows...
into a new little
Prince with a
pea for a nose!

Tulle
Brives
BORDEAUX
Dordogne
Sarlat
MONTAUBAN
Cahors
Agen
Rodez